Disney PRINCESS

Royally Fierce

The Official Disney Fan Club

D23.com

Title hand-lettering by Emeli Juhlin
Design by Lindsay Broderick

First Hardcover Edition, April 2020
Library of Congress Control Number: 2019953943
1 3 5 7 9 10 8 6 4 2

ISBN 978-1-368-04915-3
FAC-034274-20052

Visit www.disneybooks.com

Disney PRINCESS

Royally Fierce

WRITTEN BY *Erin Zimring* AND *Brittany Rubiano*

ILLUSTRATED BY *Amy Mebberson*

Disney
EDITIONS

LOS ANGELES · NEW YORK

Don't let HATERS get you DOWN.

YOU
deserve
DESSERT.

THE
fiercest girls
MAKE THE
wildest mistakes.

(SORRY, MOM.)

YOU

control

YOUR

story.

#SLAYALLDAY

#TBT

A girl's gotta LOOK OUT FOR herself.

Whistle
WHILE YOU
werk.

Some might
CALL YOU ODD;
the ones who count
KNOW YOU'RE
outstanding!

Powerful
IS BETTER THAN
pretty.

#BESTLIFE

#TRANSFORMATION #NOFILTER
#GLAMSQUAD #FAIRYGODMOTHERFORTHEWIN

YOU ARE A

force

OF NATURE.

Use those legs
FOR
adventure.

Side-eye is WORTH a thousand words.

IGNORE THE NOISE.

You've got stuff to do.

SURROUND YOURSELF WITH
powerful, magical women.

BUT NOT THIS KIND.

#IWOKEUPLIKETHIS

#GIRLBOSS

A good shoe can go a long way!

(BUT A COMFORTABLE ONE WILL SET YOU FREE.)

Always
HAVE A
bestie in
YOUR BOAT.

Shut down

THE

mansplaining.

YOUR
life;
YOUR
rules.

Be
heard.

#ALLTHEFEELS

#MAKEOVERFAIL

You know
WHAT YOU WANT.
Fire away!

YOU ARE

more than

WHAT YOU SEE IN

the mirror.

#SHORTHAIRDONTCARE

#CURLYHAIRDONTCARE

#MESSYHAIRDONTCARE

Express yourself.

Express yourself

force

Side-eye

#BESTLIFE

DESSERT

girl

YOUR
story

fiercest girls

more than

Shut down the
mansplaining

#ALLTHEFEELS

HATERS

pretty

#SLAYALLDAY

Fire away

YOUR rules

be heard

bestie

#GIRLBOSS

werk

outstanding

Adventure

good shoe

#MESSYHAIRDONTCARE

IGNORE THE NOISE

powerful